Lady Mary and The Aliens

And Other Stories

Eleanor R DeWoskin

Published by G.L. Design, Boulder, Colorado, USA

Lady Mary and the Aliens and Other Stories, 1st Edition

Copyright © 2003 by Eleanor R DeWoskin
Manufactured in the USA
All rights reserved. No part of this book may be reproduced in any form or by any electronic or mechankcal means including information storage and retrieval systems without permission in writing from the publisher, except by a reviewer, who may quote brief passages in a review.

Library of Congress Control Number: 2010913175
ISBN: 1-933983-11-6
ISBN Complete: 978-1-933983-11-0
Cover Art: Eleanor R DeWoskin
Published by G.L. Design, Boulder, Colorado, USA

Table of Contents

Lady Mary and the Aliens	5
Celeste	23
George and Abigale	45
Friends	71
Pinky Pig	89
Edna	109
Innocence and the Snake Man	133
Patricia Ladybug	153
Two Knights	173
Pweshus Finds a Home	187
Two Little Bears and the Anteater	201
Oscar the Lizard	219

Lady Mary and the Aliens

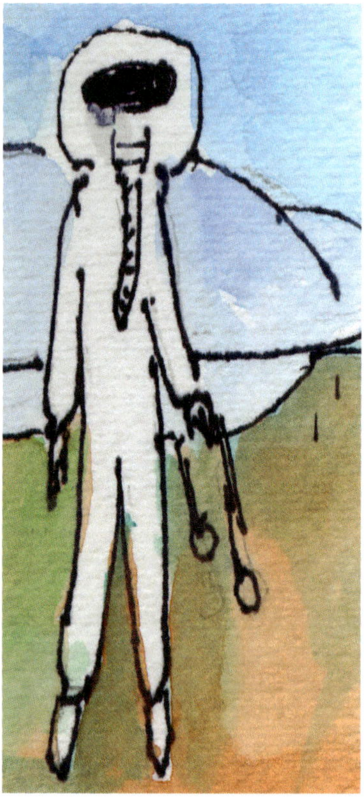

In Hawaii flying saucers are attracted to the crater of an extinct volcano. They recharge their batteries there and meet friends.

The saucer people are very shy and land at night so they are rarely seen.

Lady Mary of Goosegobble, Yorkshire was curious and, on a trip to the Pacific, rode into the desolate crater leaving her bodyguards outside.

She was the epitome of good manners and propriety but she almost bolted when a saucer flew in and circled as it settled down and landed.

Out of it stepped a tall, slender figure wearing a white coverall and an enormous white helmet.

Lady Mary was about to run from the scene when the creature spoke in a cultivated voice, "I beg your pardon for intruding but can you tell me where I am?"

Lady Mary rallied. "This is the planet Earth and we are in Hawaii. Welcome."

"Thank you. I'm Erlinger from Space Heaven."

He took off his helmet and, to her horror, he had two heads. Neither one was handsome but they were both attractive.

Lady Mary was in shock as they introduced themselves as Anthony and Andre. "How do you do?" She babbled. "I'd be de-delighted if you would come for t-t-t-tea."

"We'd be de-delighted too." they said. "What time?"

They washed their faces and brushed their teeth and by then it was time to go.

Lady Mary's parents and grandparents liked Andre and Anthony. "They are unusual but, oh, so charming" was her grandmother's verdict.

Lady Mary was squeamish about allowing Anthony and Aaron both in her bedroom and bath. So marriage was out of the question. A husband was one thing, but a witness? No way!

She was rather depressed by events and started nibbling and snacking. She became best friends with the chef and hung around the kitchen. He was good looking and fun to be with. They fell in love.

Lady Mary was too young to be serious about love but he thought she was cute and gave her goodies to eat. Meanwhile Anthony and Andre fell in love with Siamese twins.

When she was old enough Lady Mary married the chef and it was perfect except that she couldn't resist his cooking and got much too fat. He didn't mind and took it as a compliment to his cooking.

That's all

Celeste

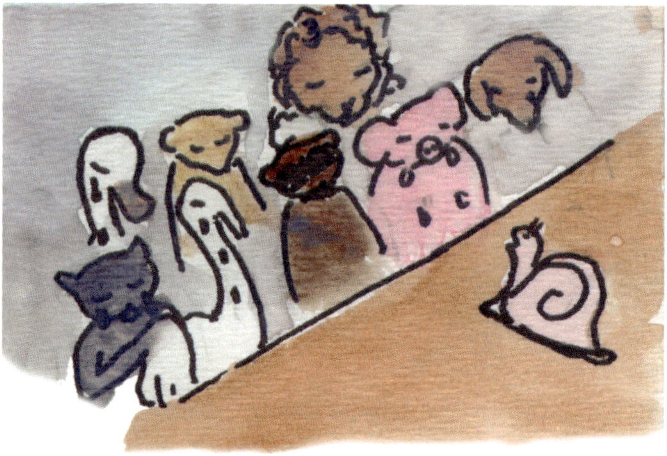

A snail named Celeste was the possessor of a sublimely pure soprano voice of seemingly infinite flexibility.

Discovered by a vocal coach, she learned voice control and the rosy iridescence of her shell made her an appealing leading lady.

Celeste often reduced the audience to tears when she played the pathetic Mimi in LaBoheme.

It was inevitable that members of the opposite sex would be drawn to her and, at the same time, be jealous of any attention she paid to others.

They were even jealous of her friendship with a lonely mole that was completely blind.

The mole, Arturo, was a long way from his native Mexico and Celeste's singing comforted his sad and lonesome soul.

Mlle Celeste

**Sunday
8pm
$20**

Now, Celeste, who was no fool, decided to charge for her singing and also put out a cup for donations from casual passers by.

She did surprisingly well and was soon settled in an apartment in a luxury high rise.

She didn't forget Arturo and it was through him that she hired an iguana to carry her about because snails have no feet and the pavement irritated her delicate underparts.

Meanwhile, her popularity soared until no other soprano was as well known and in such demand. Celeste was famous.

Celeste thought to herself "It's hard for me to imagine that a snail as lowly as I could be plucked from a rose bush and attain such fame."

Arturo agreed and told her that it was equally hard for him to fathom how she had befriended a little mole.

"*It was so easy*" she said. "*You are so outgoing and yet so gentle. You generously fulfill a very real deep need of mine for a true friendship.*"

"It is my pleasure" he replied. "Most of our above-ground friends, like the weasels, turn out to be our enemies. They pretend to be friendly and then they eat us."

"How despicably devious!" exclaimed Celeste.

The mole continued "You snails had better watch out for a snail-eating bird but, more alarming is a huge two-legged creature, hairless except on its head, that cooks and eats snails."

"I'll be careful" promised Celeste. She avoided predators as friends and cultivated vegetarians such as sheep and rabbits and squirrels.

In the end she found she enjoyed a quiet life and, except for her singing was pretty much a recluse.

Arturo also liked quiet life and retreated to his underground tunnels where his blindness was not a handicap. They talked on the phone every once in a while to keep in touch.

That's All

George and Abigale

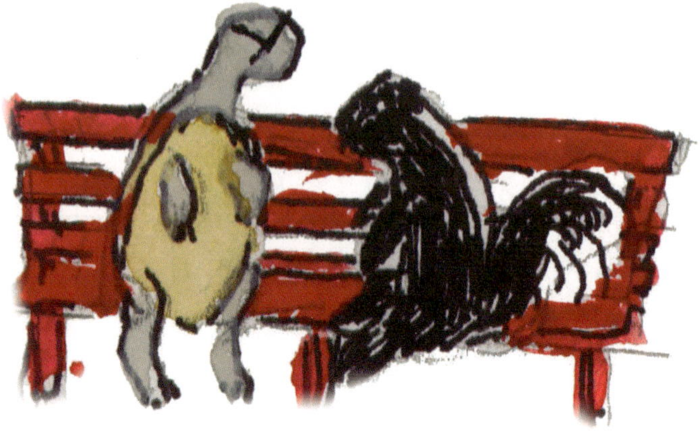

In the beginning there was a tortoise named George

whose best friend was a rabbit whose name was Elizabeth.

They had many happy hours playing together.

They were evenly matched because she had stubbed her toe and he had four wheels and goggles.

Best of all they liked to meet for breakfast, lunch, snacktime and dinner.

This was fine until one day George suggested that sharing a house would be a good idea.

They found a one story house and hired a strange creature, a monkey doodle, to saw it in half.

George chose the West half and Elizabeth the East which seemed like a reasonable arrangement

But as the summer progressed the Western sun grew so hot and strong that George felt sick from the heat.

All he could do was take long siestas and sit there unable to do anything so he got behind in his work which became a really big problem.

Worried, George went to Elizabeth and asked her to trade sides with him. She said "Nothing doing."

She was writing a novel and did her best work in the garden under the morning sun and she did not intend to be moved.

George was upset and accused her of being selfish. At the very least, she had the better deal so she should pay more. Then he could afford an air conditioner.

So again he asked Elizabeth and again she said "Nothing doing!"

George moved out and left her with all the expenses. He moved in with his sister and slept on her sofa.

Then he tried living with a family of snakes but their slithering about made him nervous.

George felt very lonely but just as it is darkest before the dawn his worst moment was just before he met Abigale, a lovely little lady skunk.

He confided his feelings to her whereupon she said she had a spare room in her house and needed a handyman to live there for room and board in exchange for help he could give around the house.

Also she had a television and, best of all, an air-conditioner. George moved in the next day.

They became friends and one day their eyes met as never before. They really appreciated each other and realized their friendship had grown into love.

So they married and lived happily until they quarreled.

...*about who got to sleep on the bathroom side of the bed.*

It got so bad that they separated. The tortoise went to Timbuctoo and Abigale went to Bali where she stood out as the one and only skunk.

That's all

Friends

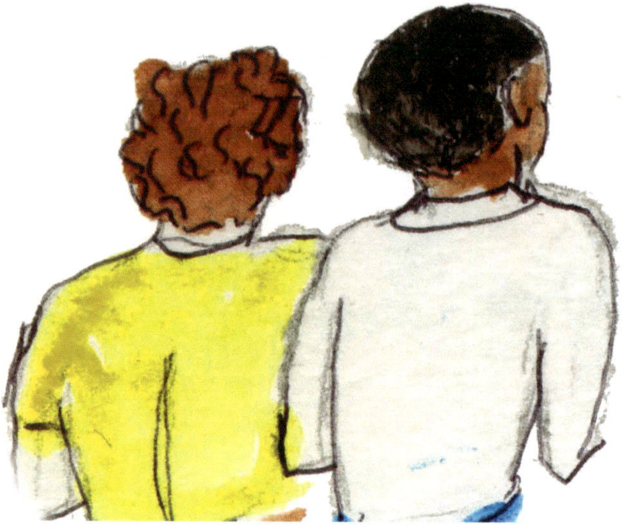

There were two back yards with a fence between them.

One one side lived a family of a mother, a father, a boy and a baby girl. They had brown skin.

On the other side lived a family of a mother, a father, a boy and a baby girl. They had a kind of pink skin.

The little boys played together and were best friends. Their fathers worked together on a 'project' so they wanted a 'project' too.

"I know" said Aaron, the brown boy, "let's raise chickens and sell the eggs."

Michael, the other boy, agreed.
"We'll get rich and buy a pony.
No, two ponies."

"We can buy two gliders and go gliding together. Then we can ride the ponies. Let's get the chickens."

They bought a batch of baby chicks. They grew into little roosters and hens.

"Roosters don't lay eggs and we still have to feed them."

"Sell them" said their fathers.

"Oh no!" The boys cried. "They'll be butchered. Let them stay." After a while the hens laid eggs that sold but buying rooster food used the money.

So they held on and, at least, didn't lose money until the hens grew old and stopped laying.

"We don't get enough eggs. What do we do?"

"Sell the old hens" their fathers advised.

"Oh no! They'll be killed." The boys protested.

"Then don't complain," said their fathers. The boys didn't complain and were happy that all the chickens were alive and well.

They never did go gliding together or get ponies and their 'project' didn't work out but they were always best friends.

That's All

Pinky Pig

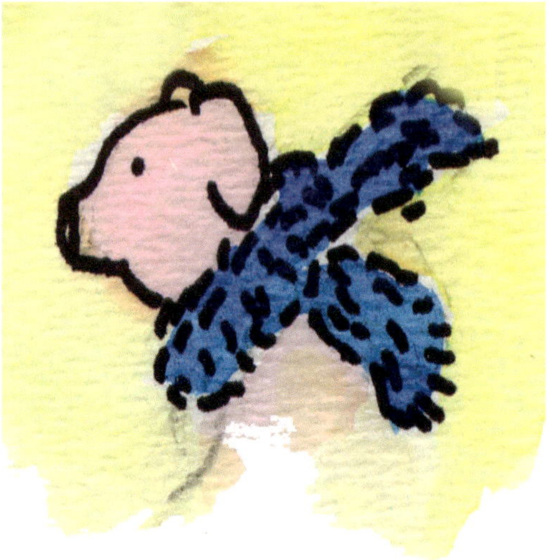

There was a lady pig that thought she was beautiful. When it was suggested she go to Weight Watchers she was insulted.

When a dress department clerk brought her a corset she was furious. She said that all modern clothes were too small for 'normal' people.

She read that in Turkey plump ladies were admired so she flew there. To her disappointment the ladies were slim and trim but she did find some second hand large harem gowns and head scarves.

She went to a dressmaker and ordered some princess and empire style dresses. They also were too small in the waist. She blamed the seamstress.

She tried everything she still didn't attract any gentlemen and was so hurt that tears trickled down her pink cheeks.

It wasn't until she met Wally, a walrus, that anyone showed a romantic interest in her. He told her she was lovely and her smooth pink body was sexy.

"You are a slick chick," he said. "Or, better yet, a slick, pink chick and not a boring gray like my lady friends.

Wally asked her for a date but, since he couldn't move about much on land, it was spent on a large boulder looking at the moon.

Pinky wasn't thrilled by their first meeting and refused a second rockbound date. "You can stare at the moon only so long before you start to act strangely," she told Wally.

"That's the fun of it" he replied.
"You might find yourself admiring my flippers someday."

"A likely story!" Pinky protested. "The day that happens is the day all the angels fly down to earth to put things in order."

Just then, there was the soft rustle of feathered wings and the sweet voices of angels singing as they landed on the earth.

"We've come to put things on earth in order," they told Pinky. For instance, you should be slender and have fur so you won't be cold in the winter.

"I don't want to be slender and covered with fur" answered Pinky. "I am beautiful just the way I am."

"In that case we won't bother you,"
the head angel said and off they flew.

This left Pinky in her overstuffed body. She never found a gentleman friend but she did adopt some baby foxes and taught them to work for a living and leave chickens alone.

The chickens gave Pinky a blue feather boa that she wore to formal affairs. She thought it made her even more beautiful than Nature had made her. Her admirers agreed.

That's all

Edna

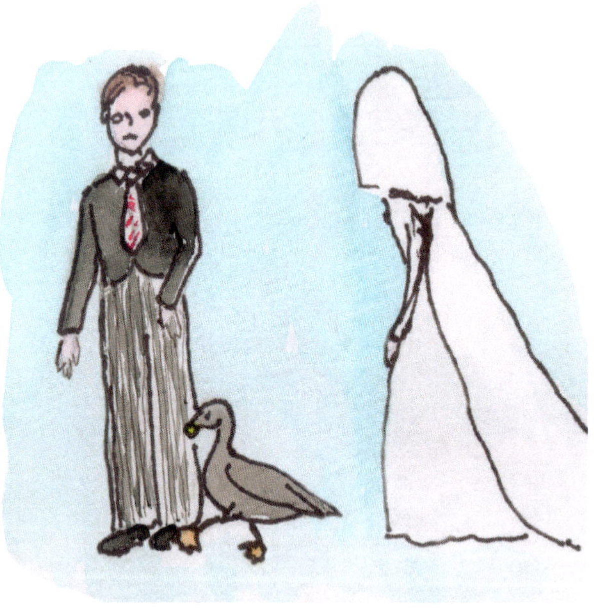

There was a little witch named Edna. Edna had problems. First of all, she was tiny, and second, she had red hair and freckles and a little turned-up nose.

Edna didn't look like a witch. However, she also had many powers, one of them being the power to assume different forms. She could be a cat by the fireplace in winter.

Or an Arctic Seal in the hot summer.

Or a Southbound Goose in the fall.

It was as a goose that she first saw Joseph. He had brought a group of children to the lake where she was living and his good looks and kindness won her heart.

Edna was in love. She thought Joseph might not like a witch so she remained a goose and followed him everywhere.

He was puzzled but grew fond of his feathered friend.

One evening a robber with a gun held up Joseph. He planned to take Joseph's money and his watch and ring, but Edna interfered.

She bit him and whacked him with her wings and drove him away.

Joseph was grateful and when he married Margie, a very nice school teacher, Edna carried the ring.

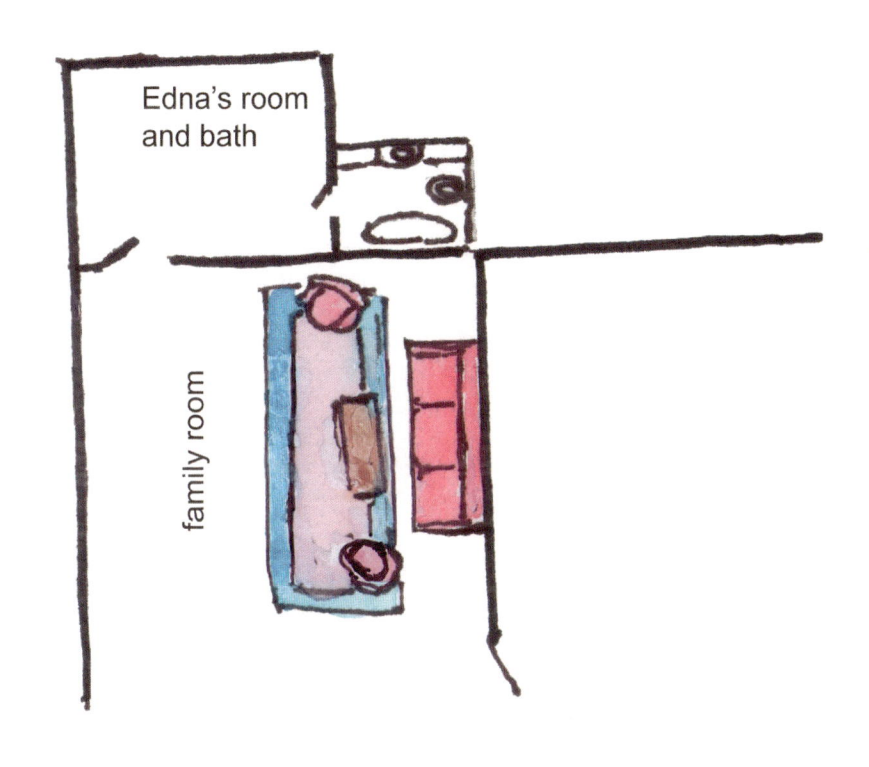

Joseph and Margie built a house with an extra room and bath for Edna.

There was a pond outside.

And she loved to float in the tub.

She learned to use the toilet.

Because the winter nights were long she took up scrabble. Edna seemed to have a gift for languages. She learned a little French.

She also liked to sit on Joseph's lap and listen to a story.

She and Joseph kept a chess game going and Edna got to be a pretty good player. She won more than half the games.

The big test for Edna came when Joseph and Margie had children. She was jealous and hid her head in a corner.

Margie had a long talk with Edna. She asked her to help her rear the children. Edna was thrilled.

Edna was an excellent nanny, and when the children were old enough, she took them for their walks.

That's all

Innocence and the Snake-Man

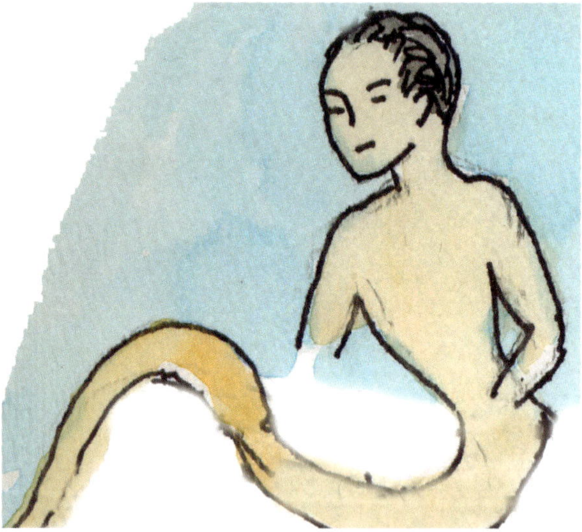

Once upon a time there lived a young woman named Innocence. She was sweet, kind, intelligent and quite pretty but unversed in the ways of love.

She lived in a little cottage in a magical forest all by herself where she studied religions and baked cookies. She was content albeit a bit lonely.

Then one day a newspaper arrived at the house and on the front page was a picture of a very handsome man-snake. Innocence was both astonished and intrigued.

His name was Mortimer Cad and the article was about what an eligible bachelor he was. He was charming, amusing, rich and interested in reincarnation.

Innocence didn't mind at all that he was part snake. She arranged a meeting and the two bonded over tea and cookies and professed their undying love.

Before long they were engaged and Innocence moved into his mansion on the south side of town. She didn't think it odd that it was also under a rock.

Mortimer was very popular with the ladies and decided to run for mayor. With all the woman's organizations working for him, he was a 'shoo-in'.

Mortimer was a good mayor and Stupidville soon became a boomtown and home to a lot of ladies of ill repute.

He found Innocence attractive and showered her with attention. She blossomed under his care and her cheeks became rosy and her long, curly hair more beautiful.

It was about then that he realized that she, although pretty, was rather boring. How could he inject some spice into their relationship?

In answer to his need the prince of the kingdom of Yawns appeared astride his unicorn. His Highness was having a yawning fit until he saw Innocence.

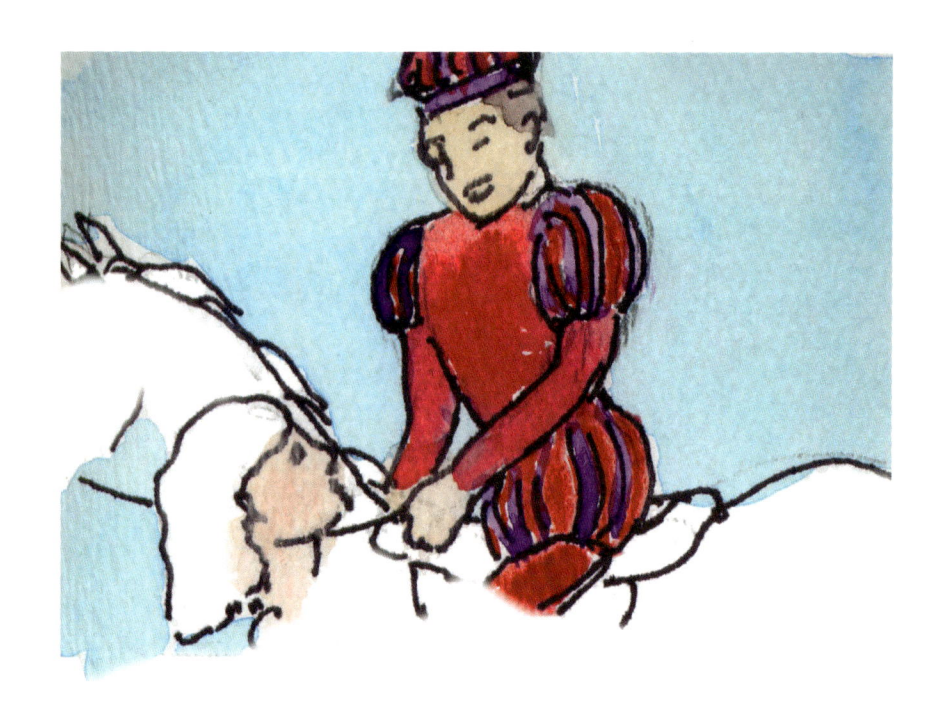

"Come hither, pretty maid," he said.

Innocence didn't like that.

"First, I am not a maid and second, I cannot be summoned like a dog."

The prince apologized. "Forgive me Madamoiselle. I didn't mean to trivialize your praiseworthy spirit of independence."

Mortimer made the same claim and said he had never in his life bedded an unwilling maiden.

After a few months of pleasing Mortimer and his highness, she realized that she was with child. Whose child? She didn't know. Was it a Cad or royalty?

After nine months she gave birth to boy twins. Not sure of their parentage, she named them Mortimer Jr. and Prince.

That's all

Patricia Ladybug

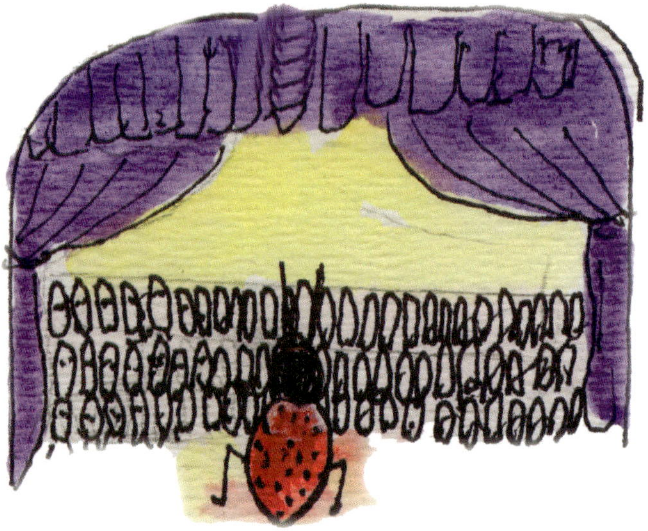

Each year at the beetle convention the members decide what their next year's duties will be.

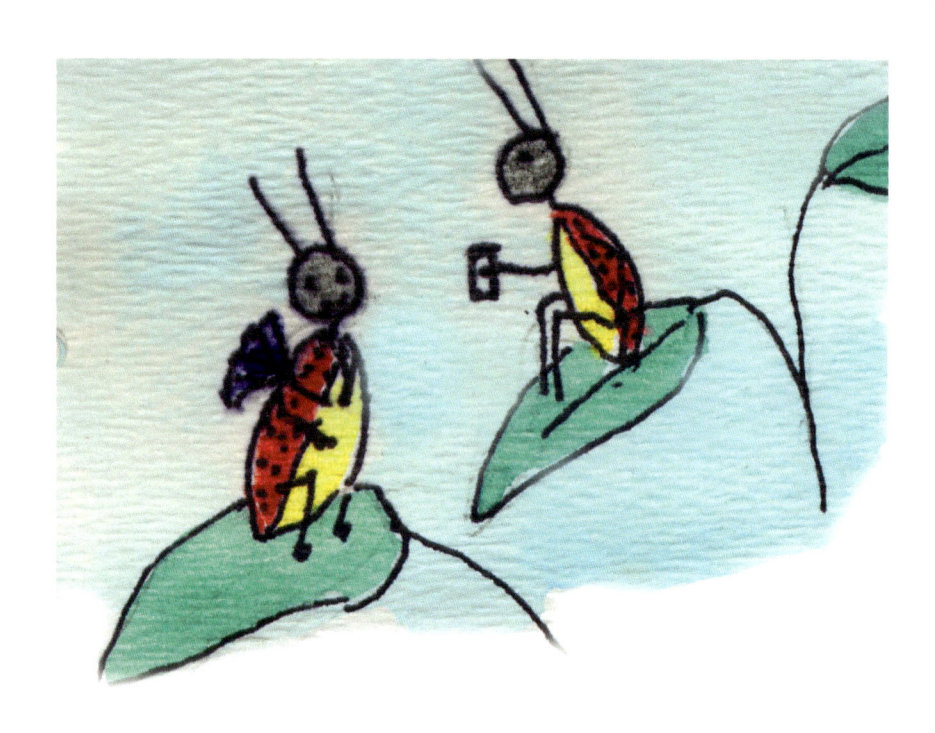

In the last meeting they voted that the job of the ladybug was to be nice ---just sitting around being cute and agreeable.

This didn't suit one little ladybug, Patricia. She was cute but not agreeable. She had a terrible temper and stamped her feet and used bad language to get her way.

The other ladybugs tried to reason with her and help her enjoy being agreeable but, no matter what they advised, Patricia disagreed.

Bad example sign

Finally, they gave up and said she could be their bad example which she enjoyed. As a bad example she could be as naughty as she pleased.

So she stirred up trouble by being so disagreeable that no one could stand her company. She was a wonderful bad example.

Patricia had one problem. When she made someone unhappy she felt sorry for them and sorry for what she had done. It took the fun out of being bad. She made a list:

<u>Bad</u>	<u>Good</u>
hurt others	help others
frown	smile
leave dishes	wash dishes
refuse nap	take nap

This didn't make her happy but she felt she had to go on being the 'bad example.' She thought that was what she was supposed to do but she really wanted to try being agreeable and helpful.

Now, ladybugs eat aphids that are tiny bugs that just sit on plants and suck the juice out of them. They don't talk or sing or laugh and are not very entertaining. They do give a very tiny scream when a ladybug grabs them.

Patricia made friends with these living in a large begonia and, encouraged by their screaming, organized them into "The Choir of 2000 voices." Together they sounded like a piccolo played by a master musician.

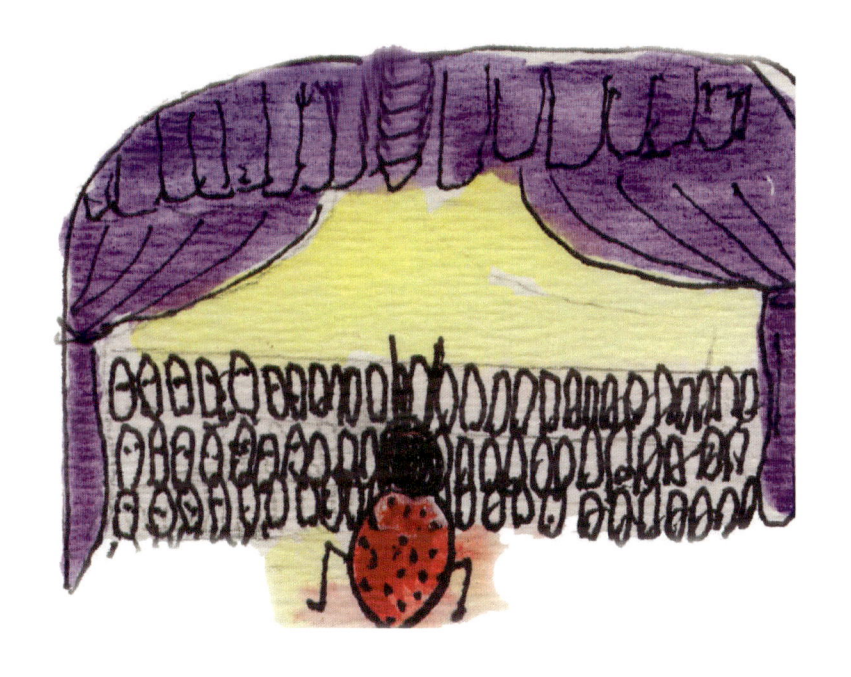

Accompanied by the New York Philharmonic they performed in Carnegie Hall. For one encore they played "The Whistler and His Dog" which brought down the house.

When Patricia added the four mockingbirds the effect was enchanting. Their song was both sweet and strong.

Crickets can also do percussion numbers and the mockingbirds were simply sublime. The concert halls of the world clamored for their performances.

She and her musicians traveled the globe leaving a trail of pleasure behind them. Patricia studied with Arturo Toscanini and began composing music.

It turned out that she was quite talented and her work was widely performed. Her opera "The Jitterbug" was a sensation.

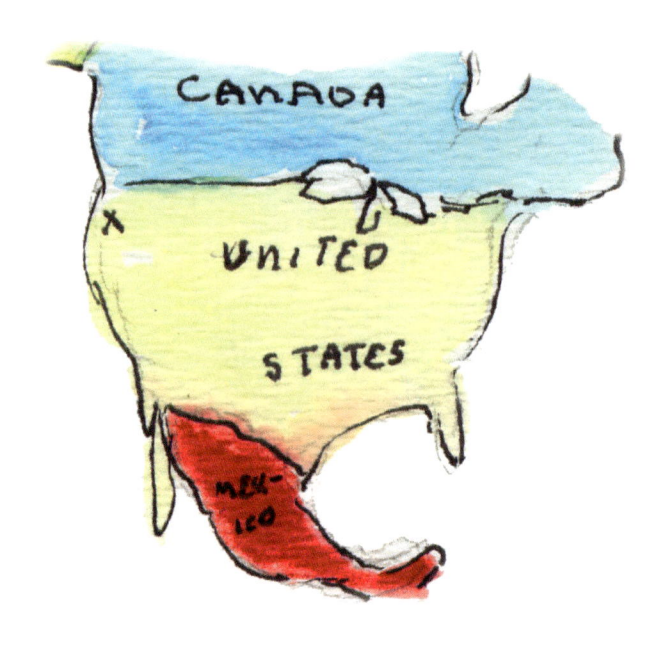

Patricia married a gentleman-bug and, the last we heard was living in Portland, Oregon, where they like the climate.

That's all

Two Knights

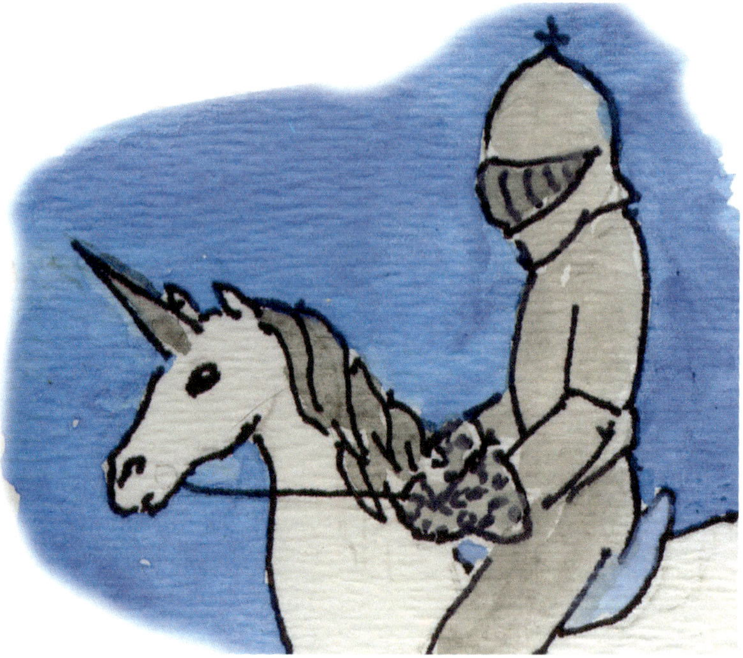

In the far away and long ago there was a land of surpassing beauty where wild unicorns roamed.

They grazed in the green valleys and drifted up the sides of the snow capped mountains.

At the dawning of the Age of Chivalry the knights preferred them as steeds. They were more nimble than the horse and more obedient.

Imagine the excitement in the capitol city when into the main square rode a knight in armor as white as snow.

He was riding a unicorn that had grown old in his service and it was time for it to retire. It's name was Vulcan.

His rider was the White Knight who was the soul of gentleness and practiced love and kindness wherever he went.

He was searching for a young unicorn to take Vulcan's place.

A flamboyant Black Knight also needed a steed. He traveled to the very Gates of Hell to buy a flame red dragon with a mane of gold.

Astride his formidable steed he returned to challenge the White Knight to a jousting tourney with lances eight feet long.

The knight's mothers told them to talk about their differences but they couldn't remember what they were.

They began to laugh about how angry they had been over nothing. Then they had a tea party with tea and toast with raspberry jam and enjoyed it.

That's All

Pweshus Finds a Home

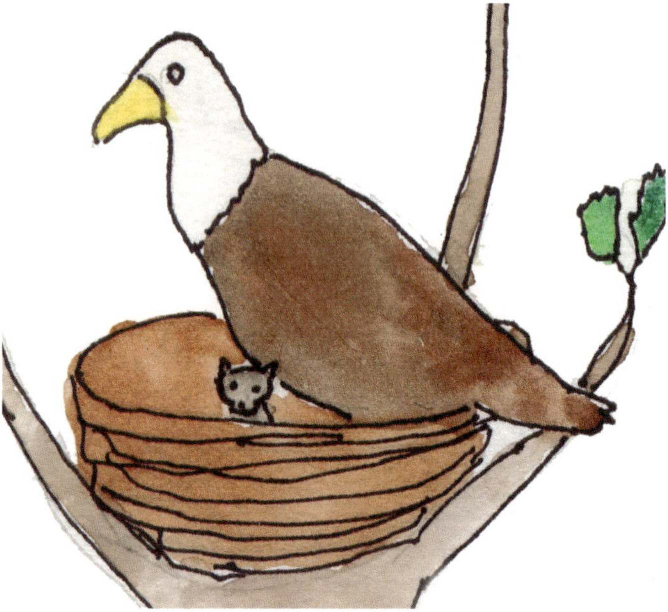

There was a kitten that was very small

His name was Pweshus and he didn't know much yet. He was still a baby cat.

He did know that he was a boycat and that he was lonely and needed a friend.
He met a chicken

that was lonely too so they decided to live together. The chicken slept perching on a pole.
Pweshus tried but he wasn't comfortable.

The chicken's name was Hariet and her aunt told her that chickens made nests.

"Up in a tree?" Harriet asked.

"I guess so," said the aunt.

So Pweshus and Hariet started building a nest in a tree.

It was scary! Pweshus was afraid he would fall out and Hariet's wings got tired. Meanwhile, the Prairie dogs dug out a lovely underground home for them.

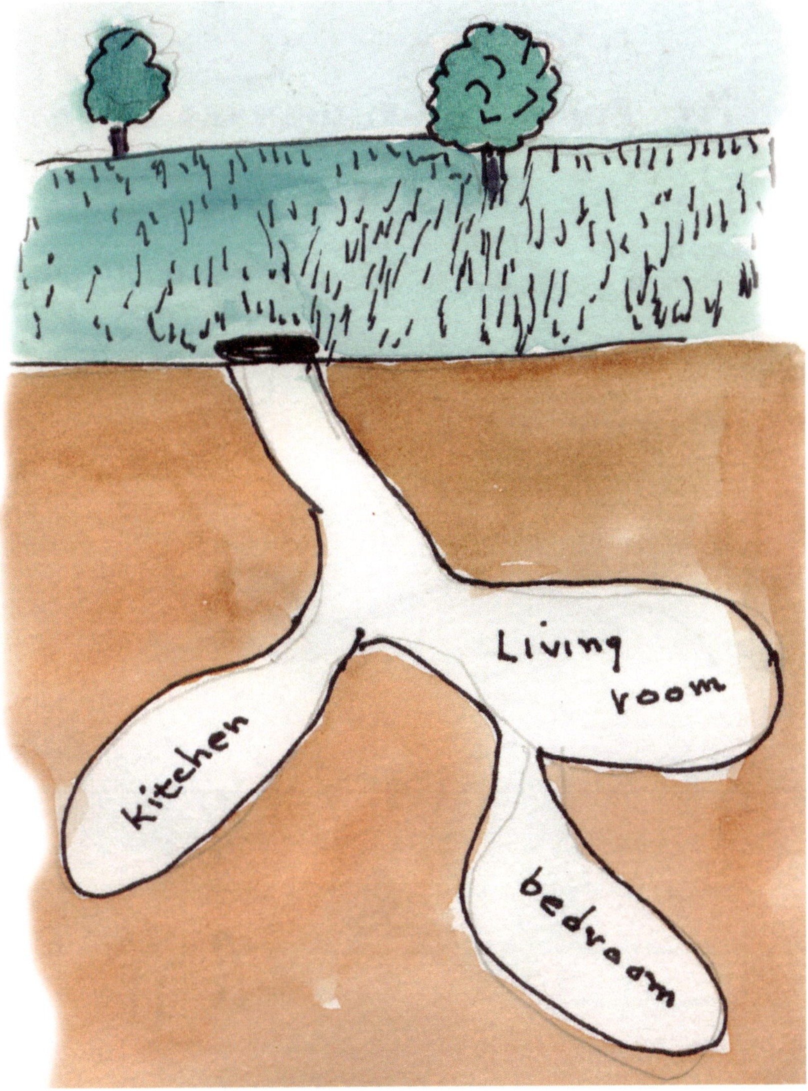
Living
room
kitchen
bedroom

Their new neighbor, Mr. Mole, ate worms and Hariet loved worms too and her scratching helped keep the earth soft. They got along well.

Pweshus had to catch his own dinner.

but he still slept in his nest.

Guess what! A great big old eagle, Major General Hossenfeffer, thought Pweshus was a funny looking baby eagle and adopted him.

Pweshus was worried but, luckily, you found him and gave him a happy home.

That's all

Two Little Bears and an Anteater

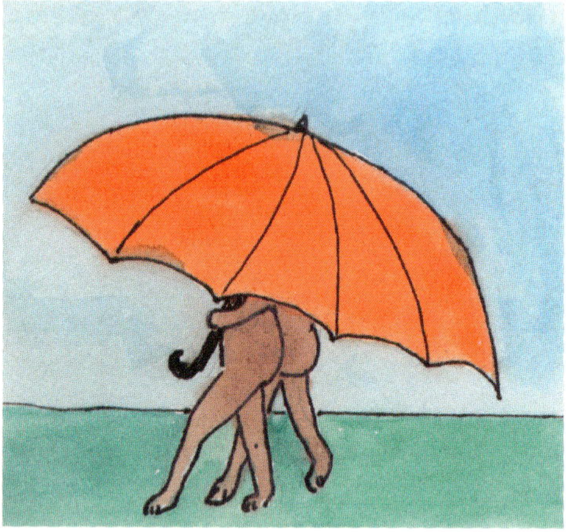

Once upon a time there were two little bears.

They lived in a cave in the forest.

They were named Billy and Bobby and they shared everything.

Food

(the food)

the umbrella

The cave

The bed

That was fine until Billy started eating crackers in bed. The crumbs felt like sand to sleep on. Bobby hated that.

Bobby thought that maybe an anteater might like crumbs so he sent to Argentina for one. "If the poor thing eats ants, cracker crumbs should be a treat" he thought.

However, the anteater, Julius, was tired of ants and the crumbs gave him a tummyache. He asked for chicken broth.

Bobby gave him broth. "You know you can't eat crumbs and there are no ants to eat. What use are you!"

"I'm good at clearing out flooded basements," *Julius replied.* "and washing dogs."

"Oh dear," *Bobby sighed.*

A passing sparrow saw Bobby and stopped to visit.

"He can't eat cracker crumbs? Strange! We birds are experts with crumbs."

The sparrow flapped his wings, which signaled to the others that he had found food.
Soon there were a lot of sparrows gathered and the crumbs were gone.

"There's a solution to every problem" said Julius. "I'll show you. I turned the basement faucets on."

"Oh, my goodness! Oh dear me!" said Bobby. "Have pity on me!"

That's all

Oscar The Lizard

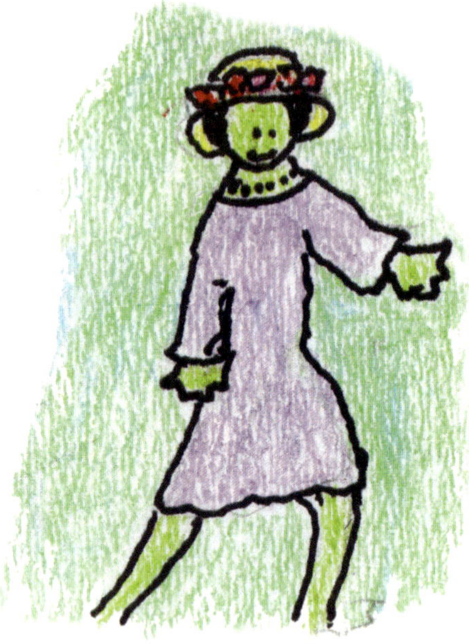

There was a lizard named Oscar who lived happily in a village of small animals. Birds woke them in the morning and crickets put them to sleep at night.

Everyone was well and happy except for Oscar Lizard who couldn't control his weight. His tummy was so fat it hung out over his belt. He went to Weight Watchers and Overeaters Anonymous but it didn't help.

That wasn't so bad except that he was in love with a young frog that had a voice like an angel's bell. She was called a Spring Peper and she chimed 'knee deep' over and over.

Oscar gave her presents and took her to dinner and the theater. He gave her pretty clothes and she thought he was wonderful. Her name was Alice.

What Alice didn't know was that Oscar was also having an affair with Hildie, a gorgeous yellow and blue butterfly.

Hildie knew something was going on, when, whenever marriage was mentioned, Oscar would say 'some day' or that he was 'not ready yet." He told Alice the same thing.

That was before he saw Annie, a small lizard with gold flecked skin and a gilded crest. He was completely enchanted by her and followed her everywhere.

Annie thought he was too old for her and said it would be like dating her father. She introduced him to her aunt and widowed mother.

But Oscar was in love with Annie and, after a long and passionate courtship, he won her hand. They were married in a 'May-December' wedding.

Before the year was over Annie gave birth to a lovely little girl lizard. She and Oscar were surprised and Oscar were surprised and delighted.

In their joy at being together they forgot to take precautions and soon they had several baby lizards.

They learned there were a lot of lizards in the Grand Canyon and the desert South West

Most importantly, they used birth control and Oscar was elected to the National Board of Planned Parenthood.

Oscar read about the 'outback' in Australia and decided it would be an ideal place to start a new lizard colony. Things were getting rather crowded in the USA.

Peru was another possibility but it was whispered that the natives were fond of a lizard-potato chowder. Also the mountains were higher than Alice, Hildie and Annie liked them to be.

Oscar talked to the captains of some ships about immigrating but they said they'd be damned if they'd take a boatload of lizards anywhere.

In the end they bought plane tickets to Australia. To everyone's astonishment the plane shot up like a rocket and disappeared in the stratosphere and was never heard from again.

That's all

Author's Biography

Eleanor DeWoskin, who passed away in 2008 at the age of 93, had become known as one of Boulder, Colorado's local sages. Every day she created her poems, stories and artwork while enjoying a constant stream of visitors who came by to see what she might be working on and to absorb some of her endless good cheer. When asked for advice, she usually replied, "Don't worry about it." Something about the way she said this helped people move on to the bigger pictures in their lives.

Her books contain fragments of Eleanor's natural wisdom captured from different chapters in her own life stretching all the way back to grade school. Eleanor was what her father, a professor of biology, called "range-reared." That means that she didn't have to suffer through the imprinting process called "school" which, some might claim, has a way of ironing out a person's more interesting wrinkles. Eleanor survived intact, complete with her own assortment of lovingly assembled works of art which are her unique commentaries on her journey through life.

By the age of 19, Eleanor had worked her way into the position of writer and editor for a New York magazine called "The Delineator" which eventually was purchased by the publisher of "Ladies Home Journal." The fact that she had spent her childhood running barefoot in the woods did not inhibit her avidly-aquired worldly education.

Eleanor Ritchie DeWoskin was born in 1915 in Williamsburg, VA, as Mary Eleanor Ritchie. She subsequently lived in Flemington, NJ, New York, Florida, Columbia, MO, Washington DC, St. Louis, MO and Boulder, CO.

Correspondence relating to her legacy may be addressed to her son, Cameron Powers
Email: cameron@rmi.net

Other Books
by Eleanor R DeWoskin
Published by G.L. Design
www.gldesignpub.com

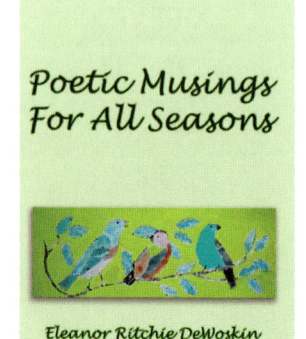

Poetic Musings For All Seasons
$16.95
ISBN13: 978-1-933983-04-2

Literally, these Poems For All Seasons, reveal a sensitive and wise personality. There is a poem for everyone somewhere in this 120 page book.

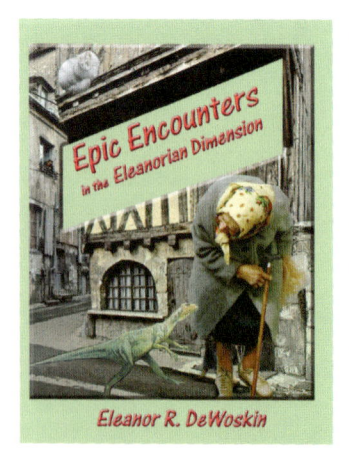

Epic Encounters
in the Eleanorian Dimension
$64.95
ISBN13: 978-1-933983-09-7

Eleanor's improbable and zany but ultimately sane combinations of images are collected in this 130 page book of full color collages.